KU-488-787

Shoo Rayner

ROMAN
BRIT

FIGHTING FORUM

ORCHARD BOOKS
338 Euston Road, London NW1 3BH
Orchard Books Australia
Level 17/207 Kent Street, Sydney, NSW 2000

First published in 2015 by Orchard Books
ISBN 978 1 40833 462 1

Text © Shoo Rayner 2015
Illustrations © Shoo Rayner 2015

A CIP catalogue record for this book is available from the British Library.

1 3 5 7 9 10 8 6 4 2

Printed in Great Britain

Orchard Books is an imprint of Hachette Children's Group
and published by The Watts Publishing Group Limited, an Hachette UK company.

www.hachette.co.uk

ROMAN BRIT

FIGHTING FORUM

ORCHARD

FORT FINIS TERRAE is a sleepy backwater in the great Roman Empire. A young shepherd boy named Brit lives there with his sheep and faithful dog Festus.

It's a quiet life for Brit and his animals in the fort. But every so often, something happens to make it a day to remember!

GERMANIA

PA

ARABIA

CHAPTER ONE

"By Jove! I've never seen so much poo in my life!" Brit exclaimed, as he threw another lump on the pile next to him.

"Baaa!" complained the sheep that Brit was holding. Picking dried poo off sheep tails was not Brit's favourite job, but someone had to do it.

"A daggy bottom attracts flies and disease," Brit explained to the bleating sheep. "You should be more careful and lift your tail a bit higher!"

He let go, and the sheep ran back to join the rest of the flock.

"There you are, Brit!" rang out a shrill girl's voice. "I've been looking for you."

Brit groaned. *Just what I need right now,* he thought. *Drusilla!*

Brit's dog, Festus, bounced off to meet her as she came skipping down the path towards them.

A stocky, sly-looking boy marched along behind her.

"Hello!" Drusilla said brightly. "This is my cousin Brutus. He's come to stay for a few days. He's frightfully clever and ever so strong. He's going to be a Senator in Rome when he grows up."

Brit smiled and said hello. The sun was right behind the boy, so he could only see his outline. He certainly was big!

"What are you, then?" Brutus asked rudely. "A shepherd boy?"

Brit knew his place. He wasn't exactly Drusilla's servant, but she was sort of in charge of him. Her father was the commander of Fort Finis Terrae, so she acted like the commander of everything else – including Brit!

And Drusilla's cousin obviously thought he was in charge too. Brutus wrinkled his nose. "What is that horrible smell?"

"I'm dagging," said Brit. "I'm removing the dags – the bits of dried poo – from my sheep." He was tempted to flick a lump of poo at Brutus, but thought better of it.

"I suppose that's all a shepherd boy is good for," Brutus sneered.

Brit felt his blood begin to boil. Festus laid his ears back and growled quietly.

Brutus was worse than Drusilla! At least Drusilla respected the work Brit did. Who was this Brutus? What gave him the right to look down on him, just because he was a shepherd boy?

Brit returned Brutus's icy glare, but he didn't say a word. There was nothing he would enjoy more than picking Brutus up and dumping him in the pile of sheep poo, but he knew he would only end up in trouble. Boys like Brutus always won in the end.

"Ahem!" Drusilla coughed loudly.

The boys continued to stare coldly at each other.

"Ahem!" Drusilla coughed again. She was wearing a happy, expectant smile on her face.

Brit suddenly remembered something. "Oh yeah!" he said, and started rummaging in his bag. He brought out a parcel, wrapped in large dock leaves and tied up with twisted woollen string.

He held out the present to Drusilla, suddenly feeling a bit embarrassed. "Happy birthday!" he said, staring at the ground. "I hope you like it. I made it myself."

"You remembered!" Drusilla squealed, as she took the parcel, ripped off the string and hastily unfolded the leaves. Festus pressed his cold, wet nose into the parcel, hoping it was food.

"Oh!" Drusilla caught her breath as she revealed a small woollen lamb. "Look, Brutus, isn't it beautiful? It looks like the real thing. Brit, you're so clever!"

Brutus leaned forward and grabbed the lamb.

"Ha!" he smirked. "It's so real, there's even a bit of poo on the tail!"

"What?" Brit snatched the toy back from Brutus to check. The tail was snowy-white and clean, just as he knew it would be – not a speck of poo anywhere.

Drusilla smiled at Brutus as if to say, *And do you have a present for me?*

"Err," Brutus looked awkward. He had clearly forgotten!

"I was going to get you a present at the forum this afternoon, actually," he said, obviously thinking on the spot.

"I haven't had a chance to get you anything before today."

Yeah, right, thought Brit, raising his eyebrows and looking up to the heavens.

"I can't wait!" Drusilla said excitedly. She turned to Brit and explained, "We're going to town this afternoon for my birthday treat. There's going to be a gladiator fight! Isn't that amazing? All those huge men bashing each other to pieces... I can't wait!"

"I don't expect you'll be coming." Brutus laughed pompously at Brit. "You're probably busy making something out of sheep poo!"

Brit gave Brutus a steely stare. *I'd like to bash you to pieces!* he thought.

"Come on, Brutus," Drusilla trilled. "We'd better go. We don't want to be late for my birthday treat, do we?"

Drusilla led Brutus back to the fort. Brit watched them go. Festus growled until the pair were out of sight.

Brit got back to work, muttering under his breath. "Grr!" he huffed. "I'll show him – if I ever get the chance!"

CHAPTER TWO

Brit swept up the sheep poo and threw it behind a hedge. There was nothing left to do, so he headed to the fort to see if he was needed there.

He wasn't in a hurry, so he took his time, throwing sticks for Festus to chase and bring back.

Drusilla's birthday group were coming out of the gates, led by her father, Gluteus Maximus, who was riding a magnificent white steed. Drusilla and Brutus sat in a hay cart while several servants ran along behind.

Drusilla shrieked when she saw Brit. She waved at him from the cart.

"Can Brit come along too?" she asked her father. "Oh please, Daddy? Do say yes!"

Gluteus Maximus looked down at Brit from his horse. His eyes narrowed as he made up his mind. Brit was just a shepherd boy – he wasn't from a good wealthy family, like Brutus. But he wasn't a servant or a slave either.

"Please, Daddy?" Drusilla trilled. "It is my birthday. Brit works so hard – he deserves an afternoon off once in a while."

Gluteus Maximus was a stern commander and a fierce fighter, but when Drusilla fluttered her eyelids, his heart went all gooey. He just couldn't say no to her.

"Come along, then," he said to Brit. "Climb in the back of the cart. Be quick about it, we don't want to be late."

"You'd better follow us," Brit told Festus, as he settled into the hay.

Drusilla clapped her hands. "This is going to be the best birthday ever, isn't it?"

Brit and Brutus locked eyes and grunted.

CHAPTER THREE

Brit had always had to walk to town before, herding his sheep to sell them in the market. Riding in the cart felt like such luxury, even with Brutus making sarcastic comments along the way.

The town was very busy. The gladiator show had caused a lot of excitement. These were real gladiators, on tour from Rome! They were going from town to town, entertaining and showing off their skills. Nothing was quite as much fun as watching a really good battle!

Large banners hung over the entrance to the forum, showing gladiators slashing at each other with swords and tridents.

"That's Triumphus!" Brutus cried, pointing out a gladiator with a big helmet. "He's a hoplomachus. I've seen him before. He's amazing."

"And the other one's called Raptor," Drusilla added excitedly.

"He's just a retarius," Brutus sneered. "Retariae only have a trident and a net. He doesn't stand a chance against Triumphus!"

Brit couldn't read the words on the banner. He felt stupid and jealous all at the same time. Brutus was such a show-off!

The edge of the forum was lined with shops. Delicious smells billowed across the arena from hot food stalls. Festus sniffed and licked his chops. Brutus strutted off. A few minutes later he returned with a little drawstring bag.

"Here you are, Drusilla," he said, handing it to her. "Happy birthday!"

Drusilla gave a squeal of excitement and quickly untied the strings. She shook the bag and a little lead figure fell into her hand. It was a tiny statue of a gladiator.

Druscilla gave a forced smile. "Oh! Thank you, Brutus." She weighed the lead figure in her hand. "It's so…heavy! It's… it's just what I always wanted."

Trumpets blasted. The crowd oohed and aahed.

"Quick!" said Drusilla. "It's starting!"

Rows of seats had been placed around the edge of the forum, making an arena in the middle.

Important people like Drusilla and her father sat in the front row. Normally Brit would have to watch from the back or

climb up on top of a roof, but today he was
Drusilla's guest.

Drusilla patted the space on the bench
next to her. "Come along, Brit," she said.
"You don't want to miss the show!"

People were staring at him, looking at
his shepherd's clothes. Everyone else was
dressed in their finest tunics.

Brit felt a bit out of place. But he also felt
strangely important.

CHAPTER FOUR

Festus had found a bone. He lay down under Brit's chair and chewed it noisily, as if it was the most delicious thing he had ever tasted.

The drums and trumpets blared as the Master of Ceremonies entered the arena.

He bowed low to Drusilla's father, and then turned to the crowd.

"Friends, Romans, countrymen!" he bellowed. "Today you are about to witness the greatest fighting skills in all the Empire."

The drums began to roll. Brit could feel the excitement building in the crowd.

"Let me introduce to you…the gladiators!"

One by one the gladiators entered the arena. Snarling and growling, they shook their swords and fists at the audience. The audience cheered and booed, depending on whether the gladiator appeared to be a hero or a baddy.

The drums rolled faster and the trumpets blared louder as the more famous gladiators were introduced.

"And finally!" the Master of Ceremonies announced. "The stars of the show – Triumphus and Raptor!"

The audience were wild by now. They cheered, clapped, stamped and whistled their appreciation.

Brit had never had so much fun in all his life. He loved the tag fight, where the gladiators fought in teams. Only one gladiator from each side fought at the same time, but if they touched hands they could swap with a teammate who would take over the fight.

There was so much cheating, and the referee was always looking the wrong way.

"Ref!" Brit and Drusilla screamed together. "Look what he's doing! He's going to cut his head off!"

But, just in time, the referee turned around and pulled the gladiators apart. No one's head fell off. In fact there wasn't even any blood. But it was so exciting!

At the half-time break, Drusilla's servants bought them roast chicken buns, sweetmeats and spiced hot drinks. Brit couldn't remember when he had last tasted anything so good. The hot drink soothed his sore throat. He'd been cheering and screaming so much!

The contests continued, each more thrilling than the last, until it was time for the main event – Triumphus versus Raptor!

Triumphus, the hoplomachus, was the crowd's favourite. He was big. He was mean. He looked fantastic in his armour!

He was armed with a short, stabbing sword and a shield. Magnificent red plumes rose from the crest of his intricately decorated helmet, which covered his head completely.

Brutus rose to his feet and cheered. He sounded like a boar wallowing in the mud.

Raptor, the retarius, had much less armour. Only his right shoulder was protected, and all he had to fight with was a three-pronged trident and a net called a *rete*.

Brit decided that if Brutus was supporting Triumphus, he wanted Raptor to win.

Brit rose to his feet and cheered as Raptor punched

the air with his trident. Drusilla joined in. Raptor's face was scarred, but he looked honest and…very handsome!

The two warriors faced each other, flexing their huge, powerful muscles.

"I want a nice clean fight," said the referee. "Biting is allowed, but no killing. Ready? Fight!"

Triumphus roared behind his mask and leaped forward, trying to plunge his sword into Raptor's side. The crowd cheered as Raptor blocked the blade  with the staff of his trident. He swung his net over Triumphus's helmet. Raptor dragged Triumphus around the arena, trying to make him lose his balance.

Triumphus staggered backwards, slipped and fell to the ground. Raptor went in for the kill. The crowd booed and jeered at him.

Raptor had the points of his trident at his opponent's neck. He looked up for a second at the crowd, who were still hissing at him. He snarled back at them, not paying attention to what Triumphus was doing. From the ground, the hoplomachus planted the studs of his sandals in Raptor's stomach and heaved him high into the air. Raptor went flying, and Triumphus sprung back to his feet, ready to continue the fight.

The crowd went wild. Brit felt dizzy with the noise and excitement.

Festus couldn't bear to see Raptor being beaten by this huge metal man. He dived into the arena, barking and nipping at Triumphus's heels.

"Festus!" Brit screamed. "Come back here! You'll get hurt!"

But Festus couldn't hear

him above the noise. The crowd cheered as Festus barked and snapped at the gladiators' feet.

The fight went on and on. The crowd was getting tired, and the two men were clearly exhausted. Finally, Triumphus heaved one massive blow at Raptor, slashing his trident in two. Raptor collapsed as though his legs had turned to jelly.

Triumphus had won. The crowd had

strength for one last cheer
as the referee grabbed
the hoplomachus's arm
and held it high in
the air.

"The victor!"
yelled the referee.

CHAPTER FIVE

Drusilla looked concerned as Raptor
was carried away on a stretcher. "Can
we go and see if he's all right, Daddy?"
she pleaded.

She had that sad look in her eyes that her
father could not resist.

"Oh, come on then," he smiled.
"Follow me."

Brutus curled
his lip and
whispered
to Brit.
"Trust you
to chose the
loser!"

Drusilla's father led them to the little tented village that the gladiators had set up behind the forum. He marched in as if he owned the place.

Raptor was helping Triumphus unlock and remove his helmet.

"Ha, ha!" Triumphus laughed. "That was a good fight."

"And what about the dog?" Raptor grinned. "The crowd loved him, didn't they?"

Festus ran up to Raptor and licked his face with his long, wet, drooling tongue.

"And here he is!" Raptor laughed. "The star of the show!"

"That was so exciting, Raptor!" Drusilla gushed. "I thought Triumphus was going to chop off your head!"

"I wouldn't chop his head off,"
Triumphus grabbed hold of Raptor in a
headlock. "He's my best friend!"

Brutus, meanwhile, could hardly take
his eyes of Triumphus's magnificent
helmet. It glittered in the late afternoon
sun. Snake designs writhed all over it and
the plumes quivered in the breeze.

Brit, on the other hand, had picked up Raptor's net. He swung it around, feeling the weight of it.

"A hoplomachus will beat a retarius every time," Brutus said. "Who would want to be a retarius with just a pathetic net and trident? A hoplomachus is a real gladiator. A real gladiator has armour and a sword."

"A retarius could easily beat a hoplomachus ," Brit countered. "Skill is the most important thing."

Brutus leaned over so his nose was almost touching Brit's. "Strength wins every time," he snarled.

The two gladiators raised their eyebrows and winked at each other.

"Why don't you two fight it out and see who's right?" said Raptor. "We've got everything you need."

"He's just a shepherd boy," Brutus laughed.

"Ha! You're just scared you'll lose!" Brit replied bravely.

"I'll fight you!" Brutus snarled. "But you've got to tie your dog up. I'm not fighting him as well."

Triumphus began cladding Brutus in armour. "It's just practice armour," he explained. "We wouldn't want anyone getting hurt in training, would we?"

"Hey, this sword is just wood – it's not even heavy," Brutus complained, as Triumphus clamped a training helmet on his head. "Hey! I can't see!"

Drusilla clapped her hands. "You look magnificent, Brutus,"

Brit tied Festus to a wagon wheel with a thin piece of rope. "Stay there… and behave yourself!" he said, firmly. But Festus began chewing at the rope immediately.

Raptor smiled at Brit. "Here's your net and your trident," he said. "Good luck!"

The trident was made of wood. Where the sharp points should have been, three balls made it safe for practice fights.

CHAPTER SIX

Triumphus raised his hand. "We want a good clean fight," he announced. "No biting and no killing!" He dropped his arm as a sign to start.

Brutus charged at Brit, who quickly sidestepped out of the way, and Brutus stumbled forward. Brit bashed him on the

back of his helmet as he fell.

"Clang!" The heavy bronze helmet rang like a bell.

Brutus flailed and roared and staggered about under the weight of the armour.

With hardly anything to carry, Brit was lighter and more nimble. It was easy to keep out of the way, even if Brutus was bigger and stronger.

"Come on, Brutus!" Brit taunted. "I thought a hoplomachus could beat a retarius any day?"

Brutus huffed and puffed and charged. Brit threw his net, which caught Brutus's sword arm. As Brutus tried to free himself, Brit poked his ankles with the trident.

"Ow! Stop it!" Brutus was hopping from one leg to another, trying to avoid the ends of the trident.

Finally, Brit poked Brutus in the back of the knee. Brutus's legs crumpled and he crashed heavily to the floor.

Brit gently placed the prongs of his trident on Brutus's neck.

Brit leaned close to the helmet so Brutus could hear. "So… can a retarius beat a hoplomachus?"

Brutus made a grunting noise from inside the helmet.

"Sorry…" Brit grinned. "I couldn't hear that."

Everyone strained to hear Brutus's weak, echoey voice.

Festus chewed through the last thread of string. He wanted to join in the game. He bounced up to Brit and began snuffling around Brutus's neck.

"Eurgh! Get him off me!" Brutus groaned. "I give in!"

Raptor slapped Brit on the back. "You were right," he said. "It's all about skill."

"And having the right people on your side," said Brit, giving Festus a huge hug.

"Never mind," Triumphus said kindly, as he helped Brutus out of his armour. "You'll get nice and fit when you join the army."

"I'm not going to join the army!" Brutus grumbled. "I'm going to be a Senator in Rome!"

"That's probably a very wise decision, sir." Triumphus laughed and bowed in a mock salute.

Later that evening, Drusilla's birthday group were making their way back home. Festus had been allowed to ride along with them in the hay cart. Brutus was fast asleep, grunting and snoring.

Drusilla could hardly keep her eyes open anymore. "That was the best birthday treat ever," she said sleepily. "You were so clever defeating Brutus like that. He can be a bit pompous, can't he?"

Drusilla sighed. Her eyes drooped and fluttered shut. Brit pulled a sheepskin over

her to keep her warm. He noticed she was hugging the little sheep he had made for her.

The late evening sun had almost sunk below the distant hills, and blood red clouds streaked the golden sky.

For a tiny moment Brit thought of Drusilla as a friend. But the moment passed. *She'll be the same old bossy-boots tomorrow,* he thought.

Brit put his arm around Festus and sank into the warm hay. "At least I have you, Festus."

Festus gave him a great big, wet, sloppy lick and settled down next to him. It had been a very busy day!

ROMAN
BRIT

COLLECT THEM ALL!

GRIZZLY GLADIATOR   978 1 40833 454 6

BALLISTIC LOGISTIC   978 1 40833 449 2

STINKIUS MAXIMUS   978 1 40833 446 1

BOAR WARS   978 1 40833 456 0

FIGHTING FORUM   978 1 40833 462 1

DEAD HEAT   978 1 40833 465 2